For Henry

HOLLY HOBBIE

The Night
Before Christmas

POEM BY CLEMENT C. MOORE

LITTLE, BROWN AND COMPANY
NEW YORK • BOSTON

'*Twas the night before Christmas,* when all through the house
Not a creature was stirring, not even a mouse.
The stockings were hung by the chimney with care,
In hopes that St. Nicholas soon would be there.

The children were nestled all snug in their beds,
While visions of sugarplums danced in their heads,
And Mamma in her kerchief, and I in my cap,
Had just settled down for a long winter's nap,

When out on the lawn there arose such a clatter,
I sprang from the bed to see what was the matter.
Away to the window I flew like a flash,
Tore open the shutters and threw up the sash.

The moon on the breast of the new-fallen snow
Gave the luster of midday to objects below,
When, what to my wondering eyes should appear,
But a miniature sleigh, and eight tiny reindeer,

With a little old driver, so lively and quick,

I knew in a moment it must be St. Nick.

More rapid than eagles his coursers they came,

And he whistled, and shouted, and called them by name:

"Now, *Dasher*, now, *Dancer*! Now, *Prancer* and *Vixen*!

On, *Comet*! On, *Cupid*! On, *Donder* and *Blitzen*!

To the top of the porch, to the top of the wall!

Now dash away, dash away, dash away all!"

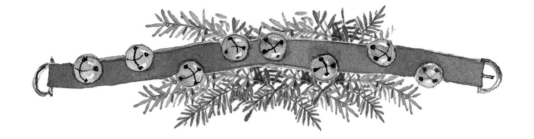

As dry leaves that before the wild hurricane fly,
When they meet with an obstacle, mount to the sky,
So up to the housetop the coursers they flew,
With the sleigh full of toys, and St. Nicholas too.

And then, in a twinkling, I heard on the roof
The prancing and pawing of each little hoof.

As I drew in my head and was turning around,
Down the chimney St. Nicholas came with a bound.

He was dressed all in fur, from his head to his foot,
And his clothes were all tarnished with ashes and soot.
A bundle of toys he had flung on his back,
And he looked like a peddler just opening his pack.

His eyes—how they twinkled! His dimples how merry!
His cheeks were like roses, his nose like a cherry!
His droll little mouth was drawn up like a bow,
And the beard on his chin was as white as the snow.

The stump of a pipe he held tight in his teeth,
And the smoke, it encircled his head like a wreath.
He had a broad face and a little round belly
That shook when he laughed, like a bowlful of jelly.

He was chubby and plump, a right jolly old elf,
And I laughed when I saw him, in spite of myself.
A wink of his eye and a twist of his head
Soon gave me to know I had nothing to dread.

He spoke not a word, but went straight to his work,
And filled all the stockings, then turned with a jerk,

And laying his finger aside of his nose,
And giving a nod, up the chimney he rose.

He sprang to his sleigh, to his team gave a whistle,
And away they all flew like the down of a thistle.

But I heard him exclaim, as he drove out of sight,

"Merry Christmas to all,

and to all a good night."

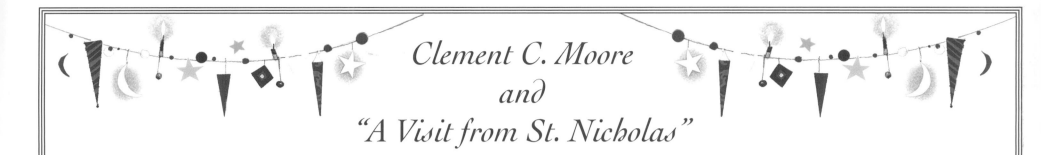

Clement C. Moore
and
"A Visit from St. Nicholas"

Clement C. Moore was born in 1779 in what is known today as the Chelsea neighborhood of New York City. He was an only child who was homeschooled until he began attending Columbia College, from which he graduated in 1798. He later worked as a professor at the General Theological Seminary and spent much of his time writing about politics, language, and religion. He could not have suspected that a poem he crafted for his family would eventually become one of the best-known pieces of Christmas literature of all time.

According to legend, Moore's inspiration for the poem was the sound of jingling bells on his sleigh. He modeled St. Nicholas on a Dutch handyman who worked at Moore's family home, as well as on the historical St. Nicholas, who was best known for rescuing children and protecting ships at sea. On Christmas Eve in 1822, Moore transformed these men into a jolly character who rode upon a flying sleigh.

A woman named Harriet Butler heard about the poem from Moore's children and submitted it to the *Troy Sentinel*—a New York newspaper—where it was published anonymously under the title "Account of a Visit from St. Nicholas" on December 23, 1823. The poem has since been published in countless newspapers, school readers, anthologies, and single editions. Moore, however, didn't take credit as the author until 1844, when he included it in *Poems*, a collection of his poetry. He has since been recognized as the author of "A Visit from St. Nicholas," now best known as "The Night Before Christmas." Some scholars claim Moore should not have taken credit for the poem, insisting that another man, Henry Livingston Jr., is the real author. To this day, Livingston's descendants work to prove the claim.

Moore died in 1863 in Newport, Rhode Island, at the age of eighty-three. He is buried in Trinity Cemetery in New York City, where each December children and adults gather to read "A Visit from St. Nicholas," sing carols, and walk in a candlelit procession to lay a wreath at the poet's grave.

Artist's Note

The prospect of illustrating a long-revered classic is intimidating. You must honor the timeless quality of the piece while somehow making it your own. Clement C. Moore's famous poem presents an all-the-more-daunting challenge because it has been celebrated by such a wide spectrum of accomplished artists, whose treatments have ranged from opulent to cute. I wanted my version to illuminate the poem's prevailing mood of mystery and wonder.

Brimming with hushed excitement, the night before Christmas is a magical time. The toddler is intended to lend a fresh perspective to the tale. Here's a child who gets to see the unseeable. There were many other decisions to be made: Just what should this jolly old elf look like? Should the setting be rural or urban? Do the interiors denote a contemporary or more traditional world? My home environment helped me resolve such issues. While the house may recall the past, the family is a modern one—so details like Mamma's kerchief and the father's cap had to go. In the end, despite doubts and revisions, the book has been a joy to work on. Frequently, I was transported back to the Christmases of my childhood, as well as those charmed occasions with my own young family. These memories have been my inspiration.

My work is done with transparent watercolor, pen and ink, and gouache on watercolor paper. Despite the many years I've been at this, I'm still discovering new ways of working. With each new project, I go through a relearning process to achieve the precise effects I'm after. I'm still always searching for the perfect paper, for instance, and just the other day I found a new brush, which was like a revelation—it seemed that much better—yet somehow I'd gotten along without it for fifty years.

—Holly Hobbie

About This Book

This book was edited by Andrea Spooner and designed by Patti Ann Harris. The production was supervised by Charlotte Veaney, and the production editor was Barbara Bakowski. This book was printed on Gold Sun matte paper. The text was set in Cochin, and the display type was hand-lettered by Leah Palmer Preiss.